D0554795

ALI BABA AND THE
FORTY THIEVES

Afterword by:
Betty Jane Wagner
Chair, Humanities Division
National College of Education

Copyright © 1980, Macdonald-Raintree, Inc.

Library of Congress Number: 79-27042

2 3 4 5 6 7 8 9 0 83 82 81

Printed and bound in the United States of America.

Library of Congress Cataloging in Publication Data

Daniels, Patricia.
  Ali Baba and the forty thieves.

  (Raintree fairy tales)
  SUMMARY: Retells the tale of a poor woodcutter who
discovers the secret hiding place of a band of robbers.
  [1. Fairy tales. 2. Folklore, Arab] I. Troughton,
Joanna. II. Ali Baba. III. Title. IV. Series.
PZ8.D188Al   398.2'2'0953   [E]   79-27042
ISBN 0-8393-0255-X lib. bdg.

ALI BABA AND THE FORTY THIEVES

Retold by Patricia Daniels
Illustrated by Joanna Troughton

Raintree Childrens Books

Milwaukee • Toronto • Melbourne • London

Many years ago, in an eastern land, there lived a poor woodcutter named Ali Baba. One day as he was chopping wood, he saw a strange sandstorm approaching.

Ali Baba climbed up a tree to get away. The
storm settled under the tree and forty fierce
men on horses appeared. They had sharp
swords in their belts, and heavy sacks on their
shoulders. 'Thieves!' thought Ali Baba.

Their captain stepped up to a great rock and
cried "Open Sesame!" The rock rolled aside.

The thieves carried their sacks into a big cave. When they came out, the captain said "Shut Sesame," and the rock rolled back into place. The forty thieves rode away.

Ali Baba climbed down from the tree and went over to the rock. "Open Sesame!" he shouted. The rock moved aside. Inside the cave he saw great piles of gold and jewels.

Rich cloth and rare pottery also filled the cave. Ali Baba gathered up enough to fill a sack and stepped out of the cave. When he cried "Shut Sesame!" the rock again closed the entrance.

He loaded the heavy sack onto his tired old donkey and walked home beside it, careful not to be seen.

When he got home, Ali Baba showed his wife the sack of gold. He told her where he had found it, but gave her a warning.

"This must be our secret," he said. "The thieves would kill us if they found out."

Ali's wife decided to weigh the gold. She borrowed some scales from the wife of Ali's rich brother Kassim. She said she was weighing grain, but when she returned the scales there was a piece of gold stuck to them.

Kassim ran to Ali Baba's house and forced Ali to tell him where he had found the gold. Ali told him the password to the cave.

The next day greedy Kassim spent a long time in the cave. He was so busy stuffing sacks full of gold that he didn't hear the robbers ride up outside the cave. When he heard the "Open Sesame!" it was too late to escape.

The robbers saw Kassim and his bags of gold. They were furious. Quickly they killed him and cut him into four pieces, to scare anyone else who might steal the gold.

When Kassim did not return, his wife told Ali Baba where he had gone. Ali Baba rode to the cave.

When Ali found Kassim's body, he knew who
had killed him. Sadly he took the body home
with him. He knew that Kassim had a very
smart and brave servant girl named Morgiana.
He asked Morgiana to help him take care of
Kassim's body, so no one would know what
had happened.

Morgiana went to Baba Mustapha, the best shoemaker in the city.
"If you can keep a secret, you will earn a gold coin," she said. That night she blindfolded him and led him through the streets to Kassim's house. There he neatly stitched the pieces of Kassim's body back together.

Then Morgiana took him home, still blindfolded. In the morning Kassim's body was buried, just as if he had died of a sickness.

When the thieves came back to the cave, they found Kassim's body gone. They knew they must find whoever knew of the cave and kill him.

One of the thieves saw Baba Mustapha in the market place and admired his work. "You should have seen me last night!" boasted the shoemaker. "I sewed together a body from four pieces."

"Could you show me where you did this?" asked the thief.

"If you blindfold me, I can take you there," said Mustapha. And so he did.

The thief marked Kassim's door with a cross. A moment later, Morgiana saw the cross. She knew it must be a thieves' mark, but she could not rub it off. Thinking quickly, she went around the street and marked *every* door with a cross.

The captain killed the stupid thief when he saw this. He led the shoemaker back to the house, and this time the captain remembered it.

That night Ali Baba opened the door to see a merchant and nineteen donkeys with two oil jars each. He welcomed the merchant for the night.

Morgiana needed oil, and thought to use some from the merchant's jars. When she dipped her pan in, though, a man whispered "Is it time yet?"

"Not yet!" Morgiana answered. She found oil in the last jar and went in to boil it. Then she went back out and poured the smoking oil into each jar. The thieves inside died instantly.

While Ali Baba ate with the merchant, Morgiana came out to dance for them. She carried a little dagger and a drum. Around and around she whirled, getting closer to the merchant every time.

Then her dagger flashed, and the merchant fell dead. As he lay there, Ali Baba realized that the merchant was the thieves' captain.

Morgiana got a share of the thieves' gold, and they all lived happily after that.

With your finger follow the path Ali Baba must take to find the treasure cave. Some clues from the story will help you on your way.

START

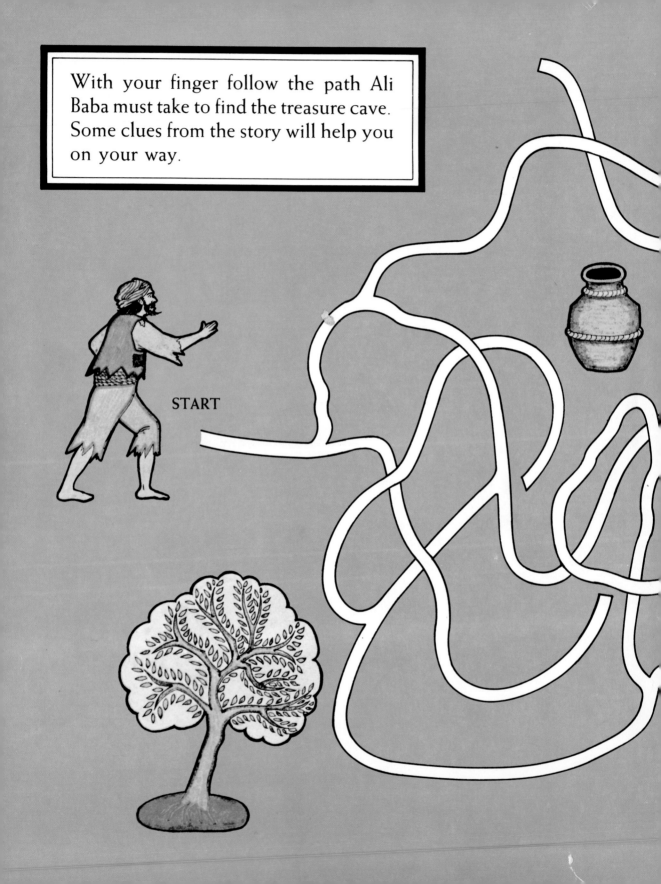

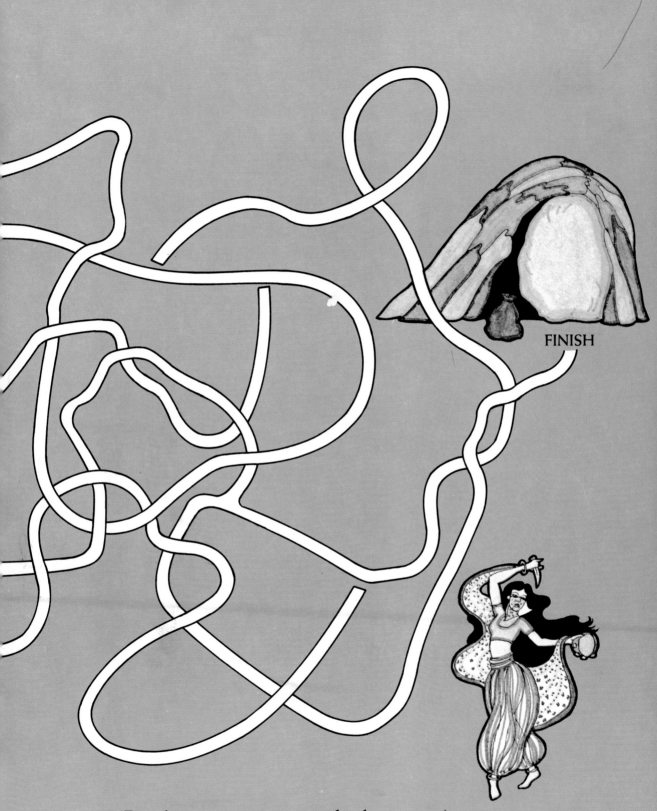

FINISH

(For the answer, turn to the last page.)

The Story of Ali Baba

"Ali Baba" was told long ago in ancient India, North Africa, Syria, and Persia. This story, like all folk tales, was told for hundreds of years before it was ever written down. When Moslem people gathered in coffee houses and in bazaars, one of them would entertain the others with the tale of Ali Baba. No one knows who first made it up, but someone who heard it retold it to someone else, and that person told it to a new group. So the story lived even after the storyteller died.

"Ali Baba", after years of being told, was finally written down in Arabia. A Frenchman, Antoine Galland, translated it into French about 275 years ago. His version was part of a very popular book called *A Thousand and One Nights*. Here are some other versions of this old tale you might enjoy:

- "The Forty Thieves", pp. 48—59, in *Arabian Nights* by Andrew Lang, illustrated by Vera Bock (F. Watts 1967).
- *Ali Baba*, retold by Jean Lee Latham, illustrated by Pablo Remirez (Bobbs-Merrill Co. 1961).
- "Ali Baba", pp. 206—222, in *Arthur Rackham Fairy Book* (Lippencott 1950).
- "The Story of Ali Baba and the Forty Thieves", in *The Arabian Nights* by Kate Douglas Wiggin and Nora Smith (Scribner 1974 c1909).

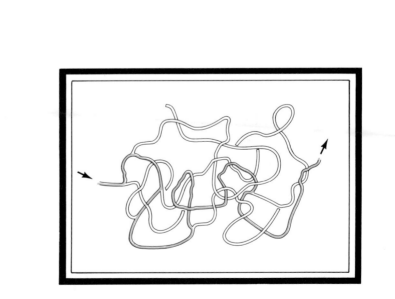

300179